THIS WALKER BOOK BELONGS TO:

_____

_____

_____

For Alexia

*There are days when Bartholomew is naughty,
and other days when he is very very good.*

First published 1993 by Walker Books Ltd
87 Vauxhall Walk, London SE11 5HJ

This edition published 2008

2 4 6 8 10 9 7 5 3

© 1993, 2007 Virginia Miller

The moral rights of the author/illustrator
have been asserted.

This book has been typeset in Garamond.

Printed in China

British Library Cataloguing in Publication Data:
a catalogue record for this book is
available from the British Library.

ISBN 978-1-4063-1184-6

www.walkerbooks.co.uk

GET INTO BED!

Virginia Miller

WALKER BOOKS

AND SUBSIDIARIES

LONDON · BOSTON · SYDNEY · AUCKLAND

It was time for Bartholomew to go to bed.
"Ba, time for bed," George said.
"Nah!" said Bartholomew.

George said, "Brush your teeth and go to bed."

"Nah!" said Bartholomew.

"Have you brushed your teeth yet, Ba?"

"Nah!" said Bartholomew, beginning to cry.

"Come on, Ba, into bed!" George said.
"Nah!" said Bartholomew.

"Nah, nah, nah, nah,

NAH!" said Bartholomew.

George said in a big voice.

Bartholomew got into bed. He giggled

and wriggled,

he hid

and tiggled,

he cuddled

and huggled,

he snuggled

and sighed.
"Goodnight, Bartholomew," said George.

"Nah," said Bartholomew softly.

He gave a big yawn, closed his eyes

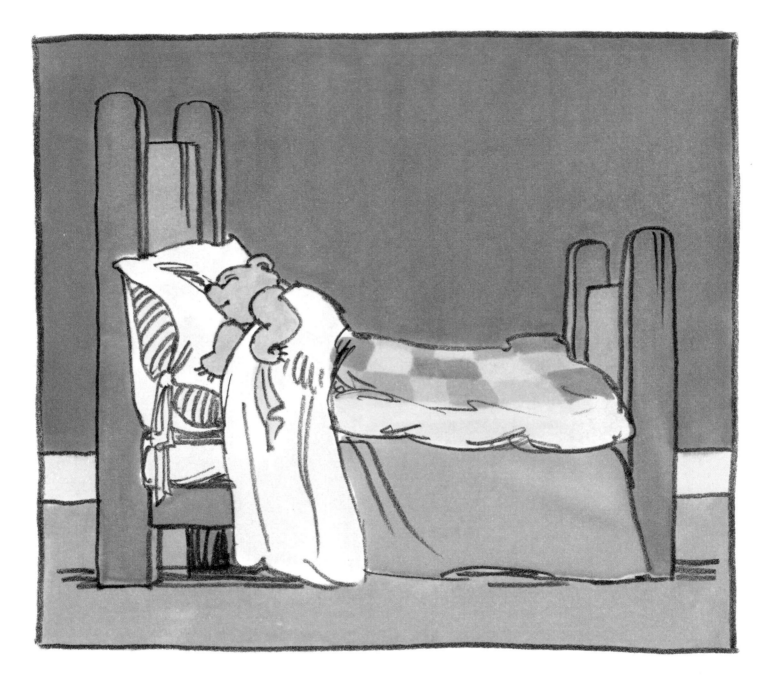

and went to sleep.

WALKER BOOKS is the world's leading
independent publisher of children's books.
Working with the best authors and illustrators
we create books for all ages, from babies
to teenagers – books your child will
grow up with and always remember. So…

FOR THE BEST CHILDREN'S BOOKS,
LOOK FOR THE BEAR